JAN   2009

Clever Katarina

A TALE IN SIX PARTS

Retold by **KEN SETTERINGTON**

Art by **NELLY & ERNST HOFER**

TUNDRA BOOKS

Published in Canada by Tundra Books,
75 Sherbourne Street, Toronto, Ontario M5A 2P9

Published in the United States by Tundra Books of Northern New York,
P.O. Box 1030, Plattsburgh, New York 12901

Library of Congress Control Number: 2005910626

Library and Archives Canada Cataloguing in Publication

Setterington, Ken
    Clever Katarina : a tale in six parts / retold by Ken Setterington ; art
by Nelly & Ernst Hofer.

ISBN-13: 978-0-88776-764-7
ISBN-10: 0-88776-764-8

    I. Hofer, Nelly II. Hofer, Ernst, 1961- III. Title.
PS8587.E835C54 2006   jC813'.6   C2005-907308-X

We acknowledge the financial support of the Government of Canada
through the Book Publishing Industry Development Program (BPIDP) and
that of the Government of Ontario through the Ontario Media Development
Corporation's Ontario Book Initiative. We further acknowledge the
support of the Canada Council for the Arts and the Ontario Arts Council
for our publishing program.

ONTARIO ARTS COUNCIL
CONSEIL DES ARTS DE L'ONTARIO

Design: Terri Nimmo
Typeset in Garamond

Printed and bound in Canada

1 2 3 4 5 6   11 10 09 08 07 06

To Dianne, the clever daughter of Vera.

– K. S.

To the outstanding teachers –
Loretta Wagler, Muriel Van Donkersgoed,
Barb Elliott – and all the teachers
who make this world a better place.

– N. H. and E. H.

PART ONE

The Wise Daughter

There was once a poor peasant who lived in a meager hut on a stony scrap of land. He had very little by way of earthly goods, but he considered himself a rich man. He was often heard to say, "I may not have gold nor silver nor fertile land, but I have a daughter. She is my share of the world's wealth." The young woman was named Katarina, and she was known far and wide because she was so clever.

One day, the king issued an order: Some of his vast properties in the kingdom were to be cleared for farmland. When Katarina heard this news, she went in search of her father. She found him chopping wood. "Father," she said, "you must go to the palace and ask the king for a piece of this land, so we can sow wheat and plant crops. Perhaps, in time, we can purchase a cow."

Katarina's father did as she advised, and made his way to see the king. "We have no land to speak of," he said, "no animals, and only a small hut. Often we go hungry."

When the king heard their plight, he took pity on the poor peasant and his daughter. "You shall have a small plot of the new farmland."

No sooner had the peasant returned home with the news than he and Katarina set out with their spades to prepare their new land for planting. They realized that, with hard work, they would soon be able to sow crops and establish a small farm.

When they had just about finished turning the soil and making the field ready to plant, Katarina's spade hit a rock embedded in the earth. A glint of gold caught her eye and, when she chipped away the dirt, she realized it was not a rock at all, but a mortar made of gold. Looking more closely, she knew that the mortar was made of pure gold. She called to her father and showed him the splendid discovery.

Her father was delighted with the golden mortar. He held it carefully in both hands. "Look at this treasure, Katarina. The king was kind enough to give us this land. We will give him this golden mortar in return."

But Katarina was dead set against the idea. She had her mother's mortar and pestle, which she used for grinding herbs and nuts. Katarina knew that a mortar was useless without a pestle. "Oh, no, Father. We can't do that! If we give the king a mortar and no pestle, he will wonder where the pestle is. We have turned up the whole field, and all we've found is the mortar. The king will think we've kept the golden pestle for ourselves. We had best keep quiet."

But her father wouldn't listen. He carefully washed and polished the mortar until it gleamed.

The next day, Katarina's father carried the treasure to the king. He told him how Katarina had been turning the soil in the field and had found it buried; how he wanted to present it to the king as a gift for his kindness in granting them a plot of fertile land. The king accepted the mortar graciously.

"I thank you, peasant, for the mortar. But isn't there something else?"

"No," replied the peasant.

"Where there is a mortar, surely there must be a pestle," said the king. "Bring me the pestle!"

The peasant wrung his cap in his hands and explained how he and his daughter had turned the whole field with their spades, but had found only the mortar.

The king was furious. "You must be hiding the golden pestle. Off to prison with you!" he cried. As the man was being led away, the king's voice followed him: "And you will stay there until you produce the golden pestle."

When the sun set and her father had not returned from the palace, Katarina grew worried. Soon enough she heard the news: Her father was in prison.

There was nothing Katarina could do to produce a golden pestle. She did not have it, she did not know where it might be, and she had no money to buy one.

Katarina was clever, so she did not despair. Instead, she set to work, turning the soil again, preparing it for planting. When the wearying work was over, she borrowed some seeds from neighbors, with promises to pay them back once she harvested her first crop.

All the while, Katarina's poor father sat glumly in a cold, dank, prison cell under the king's castle. When the servants brought him bread and water, they heard him say over and over again: "Oh, if only I had listened to my daughter. I should have listened to my daughter." The servants reported this to the king.

Then, one morning as the king was walking by the prison, he heard for himself the peasant's lament: "Oh, if only I had listened to my daughter. I should have listened to my daughter." The king was intrigued and he ordered the prisoner brought before him.

"Why do you keep saying, 'If only I had listened to my daughter'?" demanded the king.

The peasant replied simply, "She told me not to give you the mortar because, if I did, you'd demand the pestle too. She was right – you did demand the pestle! All of my friends say I have a clever daughter. I should have listened to her. She is, indeed, very clever."

The king considered the peasant's words. "Well, if she really *is* clever, then I would very much like to meet her. You can return to your daughter for now, but I want you to bring her to the castle tomorrow, so that I might see for myself how clever she is."

PART TWO

Katarina the Beautiful

*W*hen Katarina appeared before the king, her loveliness awed him. She wore no fine silks, like the ladies of the court, and her throat was bare of jewels, but her beauty outshone all the women the king had ever seen. He looked at her and smiled. "Your father tells me that you are very clever."

"It is true that some say I am clever; I hope that you will agree," said Katarina.

"I'll tell you what I will do," replied the king. "I will give you a riddle, and if you can solve it, I shall marry you and you can become my queen."

"I will try my best," Katarina said.

"Very well, then," the king continued. "Tomorrow, come to me not clothed, and yet not naked; not riding, and yet not walking; not on the road, and yet not off the road. If you can do all that, then I shall marry you and you will be my queen. If you fail, then I will send your father back to prison, and there he will remain."

Katarina smiled at the king. "Tomorrow morning, watch the road from your tower. You will see me solve your riddle." She made a graceful curtsy and left the castle with her father.

On the journey back to their hut, her father despaired. "Katarina, Katarina, what are we to do? You are clever, but the king has asked the impossible. It is not in your power to be not clothed, and yet not naked; not riding, and yet not walking; not on the road, and yet not off the road. Woe is our lot!"

"Certainly the riddle is hard, but it can be solved," Katarina said calmly, pointing to a tiny leaf that seemed to be walking along the road with them. "Who would think that a leaf could walk along a road?" She knelt down and peered at the leaf. "Look carefully. It can walk along a road when an ant is carrying it."

"Surely you are not going to be carried to the castle by ants?" said her father.

Katarina laughed. "Oh, no, but I will think of something."

When they entered their small hut, Katarina looked about. "I don't think that there is anything here to help me. I will visit some of our neighbors. I think they might have what I am in need of." As she helped her father to his chair before the fire, she noticed how thin he had become. "I will bring something back for you to eat, but for now eat this. It is the last piece of cheese we have."

Katarina left her father to his scant meal and made her way down the path. Just before she reached the river, she called out: "Father, do not worry. I will not be gone long."

PART THREE

Friends in the Countryside

Katarina smiled as she made her way to the river. She allowed herself a delicious thought. *What would it be like to be queen?* she wondered. She also wondered about the king. *Would he be a good husband to me, and kind to my frail father?* Katarina allowed herself but a sweet moment to dream before she brought her thoughts back to the king's riddle.

When she reached the grassy riverbank, she came upon a fisherman unloading the day's catch from his boat. His merry wife stood beside him, calling out to all who would hear, and to some who would rather not: "Fresh fish! Buy your fresh fish!"

As Katarina approached, the fishwife asked, "Maiden, won't you buy a fish? This beautiful fish would make a perfect dinner. A dinner fit for a king."

"Yes, I am sure that it would, but it is far too costly for me," said Katarina.

"You seem troubled, my dear," said the fishwife, kindly.

"I must solve a puzzle," explained Katarina. "If I am to keep my father from prison, I must go to the palace in the morning not clothed and not naked; not riding and not walking; not on the road and not off the road."

The fisherman looked at her with pity. "I am sorry for your father and for you, because your task is impossible."

But the fishwife smiled at Katarina. "That king is a tricky one, but there must be a solution." She and Katarina sat side by side on the riverbank, their heads together and their voices low. Soon the fishwife went to her husband and said, "We need to lend clever Katarina your old fishing net."

The fisherman laughed. "Is she going to catch the king?"

His wife shook her head and said with a grin, "Husband, just get us your old net."

When Katarina left the fisherman and his wife, it was not only with the old net, but also with a nice fat piece of fish, and many meaty fish heads besides, to make a broth to help her weakened father gain back his strength.

Katarina walked along the river until she came to a farm. It was a farm that she knew well. Many was the year she had

helped here at harvest time. A little girl saw her and called to her mother: "Mama, Mama, Katarina is here! Katarina has come for a visit."

A woman came out of the barn, carrying a bucket of warm milk. She smiled when she saw their guest. "Welcome, Katarina. Come and have a drink." She ladled out a cup.

Katarina took it gratefully and told her of the riddle. "The king has set me a puzzle," explained Katarina. "If I am to keep my father from prison, I must go to the castle in the morning not clothed and not naked; not riding and not walking; not on the road and not off the road."

The little girl cried out: "This is terrible! You won't be able to do it. Nobody can."

But her mother considered Katarina's plight carefully and, seeing the fishing net, murmured, "*Hmmm.*"

Her daughter looked at her and asked, "Do you have an idea? Can we help Katarina?"

Her mother's voice was brisk. "Well, I think that we need to find a horse or a donkey. Then we can help Katarina."

"Actually, that is why I came here. I wanted to ask if I could borrow your old horse," said Katarina.

"Oh, my dear, the horse would be yours for the asking, but the old nag died a few weeks ago. Let us go to visit our neighbors. They are kind, and what's more, they have a donkey. Besides, their donkey is a much finer beast than our old nag."

"Mama, nobody can ride that donkey. It is far too wild," said the little girl.

"How well I remember," said Katarina, with a rueful laugh. "But I must thank you, for you have given me the clue to the king's riddle." Katarina tweaked the child's braid.

"Me?"

"Yes, you. Do you remember when you tied your doll to the dog's tail?"

"Yes."

"Well, that has given me an idea. Now let's see if your neighbors will lend me their donkey."

Katarina and the woman and the little girl crossed the field and went down the lane to the next farm to see if they could borrow the donkey. An ancient farmer and his bent old wife came out to greet them.

The old couple was pleased to have guests come by, for their children were grown and they were often lonely. "Welcome to you," said the frail old man. "You must come and have tea with us."

"And I've just baked gingerbread," said his wife.

Katarina thanked them politely, but, though her mouth watered for the fragrant gingerbread, she said, "I am so sorry I cannot stay, for I must get home to my father. He is alone and he is famished."

"Tell them your story, Katarina," urged the little girl. She hopped from foot to foot in excitement.

"The king has set me a riddle to—"

Before she could go on, the little girl interrupted her: "Katarina must get to the castle not clothed, not naked, not riding, not walking, not on the road, and not off the road. If she solves the riddle, then the king will marry her and she will become queen." She finished with a flourish, "Otherwise her papa will return to prison."

The old farmer asked, "Is that right?"

Katarina nodded. "That is indeed the riddle and I know now how I must solve it. My problem is, it requires a donkey. My father and I are poor and we have no livestock, so I have come to ask a favor of you. May I borrow your donkey?"

The farmer looked skeptical, but his wife said, "This young woman needs our help. Besides, when she becomes queen, she will remember what it is like to be a poor farmer."

"I see the truth in what you're saying, wife," said the old farmer. "Go and fetch an onion or two, and carrots and potatoes." Turning to Katarina, he said, "When you return home with the donkey, remember us, and make your father a hearty soup. He must have grown weak on the water and few pieces of moldy bread he had in prison."

Katarina thanked them all – the woman and her daughter, the old farmer and his wife – and set off for home. Over her shoulder, draped carefully, was the fishing net, and on her arm she carried a basket  brimming with the makings of a good soup. With her other hand, she held the reins of a fine, spirited donkey. When she got back to her hut, her father was waiting anxiously.

"The fisherman and his wife were generous and gave us some fish, and the farmer and his wife gave us some vegetables for soup. We will have a feast tonight!"

"Never mind the soup, welcome as it would be to warm my old bones. What about the riddle? How will you go to the castle in the morning not clothed and not naked; not riding and not walking; not on the road and not off the road?"

"Oh, you need not worry about that, Father. I have an idea, a very good idea, and many of our friends have helped me."

Katarina set to work making a delicious soup. That night, for the first time in a longer time than he could remember, her father slept the blessed sleep of the well fed.

PART FOUR

A Solution
Is Found

The next morning, the king arose with anticipation. How he hoped that the lovely Katarina would win the task he'd set her, for she had already won his heart. When he looked out of his tower window, he laughed with delight. Clever Katarina had solved his riddle! The king watched as the peasant's daughter made her way up the road toward the castle.

Katarina had awakened early. By the setting moon, she'd taken off all her clothes: her apron and her shift and her threadbare dress. She'd wrapped herself in the big old fishing net, so she was not naked and yet not clothed. Then, after tying the end of the net to the donkey's tail, she bounced along, neither walking nor riding, as he pulled her toward the castle. Only Katarina's big toe touched the ground. The donkey dragged her along the grassy verge, so that she was not on the road and not off the road.

From his tower, the king saw that peasants lined the route, cheering Katarina on as she made her way to the castle. He watched her bumping progress along the roadside for a few more moments, then called 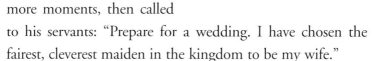 to his servants: "Prepare for a wedding. I have chosen the fairest, cleverest maiden in the kingdom to be my wife."

At the grand castle gates, he held out his hands to his bride. "Welcome, Katarina. I proclaim that you have indeed solved my riddle. I know you will make a fine wife and an even finer queen."

The people who had crowded around the entrance cheered when they heard the king's announcement. They cheered again when the king proclaimed that her father was a free man.

The marriage was held a few days later, and everyone in the kingdom celebrated their new queen. When Katarina stood at the castle entrance on her wedding day, she was much more beautiful than she had been when she had arrived wearing a fishing net.

Years passed, and with each year, the king grew more pleased with his clever wife. He gave all the royal possessions into her care, knowing that she was as honest as she was clever.

PART FIVE

A Royal Dilemma

The royal couple was happy and, indeed, so was everyone else in the kingdom. The king ruled wisely and the people loved their queen. Their contentment lasted until one unexpected day.

In the marketplace, a peasant, who had been selling firewood, found himself in a dilemma. He had brought his wood to market in a wagon drawn by three horses. One of his horses had foaled, but the little foal, with its wobbly legs, had wandered over to another stall and lain down between two oxen, owned by another peasant.

The owner of the horses declared that his mare had had the foal and, therefore, the foal belonged to him. The other peasant argued that his ox had given birth to the foal, and so the foal belonged to him. The two peasants were about to

come to blows when it happened that the king rode by. He heard the commotion and, pulling aside the curtain of his carriage, asked his steward what was causing the ruckus. The steward returned and told the king of the foal, the oxen, the horses, and the two peasants who were readying their fists.

The king thought for a moment. "Return to the peasants and tell them this, steward. Where the foal has lain, there it should stay. It belongs to the owner of the oxen."

When he heard the judgment, the owner of the mare was full of grief over the loss of his foal. Muttering and crying, he started along the road home.

When the peasant arrived back at his small hut without the newborn foal, his wife reminded him that the queen had come from a poor peasant family and that she was known to be kindhearted, clever, and honest. She told him to see the queen and ask for her help getting back his foal. The peasant saw the wisdom of his wife's words and set out for the castle. He was granted an audience with the queen.

"Yes," said the queen, "I will help you, but you must promise not to give me away. You must not tell anyone, especially the king, that I have helped you. Tomorrow, when the king is inspecting the guard, take a net, a large fishing net. Stand in the middle of the road and pretend to be fishing. Throw the net into the air and then pull it in, as if it were filled with fish. The king will ask you what you are doing and this is what you must say." The queen bent to whisper in his ear.

The next day the man stood in the middle of the road, doing exactly what the queen had told him to do. He threw his net high into the air and then pulled it in, as if he were fishing. When the king passed by, he told his steward to find out what the man was doing.

"I'm fishing" was the reply.

The steward was puzzled, but returned to the king with the answer.

The king replied, "What nonsense," and went to talk to the man himself.

"What are you doing?" the king asked.

"I'm fishing" was the answer.

The king was amused. "How can you fish, when there isn't any water?"

The peasant looked at him and said, "I have as much chance of catching fish on dry land as an ox has of giving birth to a foal."

The king was furious. "Where did you get that answer? You didn't think of it! Tell me at once where you got that answer."

The peasant replied, "I thought of it myself."

"No," said the king, "you did not think of it yourself; we both know that. Tell me where you got that answer."

The peasant was adamant that the answer was his.

"Then my answer is simple," said the king. "You will sit in prison until you tell me the truth."

It did not take many days of bread and water, and the dankness of a prison cell, to make the poor peasant confess: The queen had given him the idea.

PART SIX

Betrayal

*T*he king sent for his wife, the queen. He looked with anger and sadness at his beloved Katarina. "Why have you betrayed me? You have played me false. I cannot have a wife who will go behind my back and play me for a fool." His own words fed his anger and his rage grew. "I can no longer have you as my wife. You will return to your father's hut. You will not share my life or my castle for another moment."

Katarina looked with such sorrow upon the king that he thought his heart would break. He knew he must grant her one last kindness. "When you leave, you can take with you the best and dearest thing that you desire." He looked at her with a little less anger and said, "That is my farewell gift."

"Dear husband, if that is your command, then I will obey it." She embraced the king tenderly and, after giving him a kiss, asked if they might not share one last meal.

"Yes, indeed, it is fitting to have one final meal together," he replied.

At once the queen called the servants to prepare a feast for the two of them. She also called for a strong sleeping potion to put into the wine.

When the king and queen sat down to eat, Katarina offered a toast to the happy times they had spent together. Their glasses clinked and then the king took a deep, long drink. The queen took only a very small sip from her glass. The king quickly fell into a deep, deep sleep. Katarina called to a servant and had him bring a fine white linen sheet to wrap around the king. The servant carried the king to a

carriage that was waiting in front of the castle. Then Katarina mounted the carriage, took the reins herself, and drove them to the little hut where her father lived. She called to him to help her carry the king to her bed.

The king slept all that night and the next day too. When dawn arose the following day, the king awakened. He looked around, bewildered to find himself in a simple bed of straw with nary a servant to do his bidding. "Where am I?" he called out.

Katarina appeared at his bedside. With a loving smile, she said, "Dear king and husband, you told me that I could take that which was best and dearest to me. And that is what I did. There is nothing in the palace that is better or dearer to me than you."

The king's eyes filled with tears. "Dearest Katarina, how foolish I have been. We shall never be apart again."

He took her back to the royal castle and, soon after, they celebrated with a marriage ceremony that was much grander than their first one. Across the land, everyone celebrated once again.

From that time on, whenever the king had a difficult problem to solve, he would always turn to Katarina for advice. Together they ruled wisely and were known as the king and Katarina, the peasant's clever daughter. They had one child, a girl, who is now the queen. I have heard that she is scouring the kingdom for a clever husband.

The Art of Paper Cutting

Paper cutting had been practiced in China for centuries by the time it made its way to Europe in the 1600s. Paper cutting requires paper, and paper was, at the time, a handmade treasure. It was available mostly to the very rich or to the Church.

Monks used it for gorgeous manuscripts, decorating the texts with glowing miniature paintings and exquisite papercut designs.

Paper stencils based on Asian and African designs were lacquered or oiled so they wouldn't absorb paint and were used to decorate the walls of churches. Religious paper cuts called prayer papers were a cherished item to give and receive on holy days in northern Germany.

After the invention of the printing press, paper ceased to be a rare luxury and pattern books full of stencil designs became available. Many of the patterns that antique lovers appreciate today in furniture, embroidery, and in art can be traced back to those paper-cut stencils.

By the seventeenth century, paper cutting, or *scherenschnitt*, had become a popular kind of folk art in Germany and Switzerland, where various ways of cutting paper evolved. Some cutouts were made from single-folded papers. Others were cut from flat sheets. Color wasn't the focus – most *scherenschnitte* were cut from black or white paper – it was the delicacy and design of the shapes that engaged the artist.

People continued to find ways to use *scherenschnitte*. Professional scribes decorated legal documents with cut work, glued them to fabric or good paper, and then rolled or folded them up for safekeeping, using shapes from the original cutting to seal them. The documents were not only beautiful, but also hard to forge.

Paper-cut greeting cards and bookmarks were so popular that when people left Germany and Switzerland for North America, the cards crossed the ocean with them. We enjoy them as valentines to this day.

Paper cutting was also an important art form in Jewish culture. Often it was men or boys who worked on single-folded paper. Pictures and documents like marriage contracts were decorated with symbols drawn from the Bible.

Portuguese Jewish immigrants brought the art with them when they fled to Holland in the early seventeenth century, and it quickly became popular all over the country. The Dutch adapted the art by using knives as well as scissors to make paper carvings called *schneiden.*

Soon paper cutting was a familiar art form and the pictures included all kinds of designs and figures, not just religious themes. Colored *scherenschnitte* illustrated German fairy tales. The Danish storyteller Hans Christian Andersen also practiced the art.

Possibly the best-known kind of paper cutting is the silhouette. Silhouettes were named after Étienne de Silhouette, the vastly unpopular controller general of finances in France during the time of Louise XV. He was such a miser that his name was used for anything that was cheap. In the days before photography, when a painted portrait was a luxury, paper profiles were a way to preserve the image of loved ones. Some were tiny to fit into a locket, and others were as big as their subjects, but all of them were a source of pleasure to people across Europe.

Silhouette artists traveled from village to village, the forerunners of today's professional photographers who capture our images as important family keepsakes.

Silhouettes have given way to photography, but the art of paper cutting continues to delight. Nelly and Ernst Hofer learned their art in their native Switzerland and have passed it on to their children, Ben and Jasmin. *Scherenschnitt*'s delicacy and magic is the perfect way to make fairy tales come to life.